It's time for action.
COWS IN ACTION!

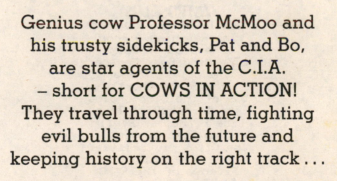

Genius cow Professor McMoo and
his trusty sidekicks, Pat and Bo,
are star agents of the C.I.A.
– short for COWS IN ACTION!
They travel through time, fighting
evil bulls from the future and
keeping history on the right track . . .

Find out more at
www.cowsinaction.com

Read all the adventures of
McMoo, Pat and Bo:

THE TER-MOO-NATORS
THE MOO-MY'S CURSE
THE ROMAN MOO-STERY
THE WILD WEST MOO-NSTER
WORLD WAR MOO
THE BATTLE FOR CHRISTMOOS
THE PIRATE MOO-TINY
THE UDDERLY MOO-VELLOUS
C.I.A. JOKE BOOK
THE MOO-GIC OF MERLIN

www.cowsinaction.com

Also by Steve Cole:

ASTROSAURS
Riddle of the Raptors
The Hatching Horror
The Seas of Doom
The Mind-Swap Menace
The Skies of Fear
The Space Ghosts
Day of the Dino-Droids
The Terror-Bird Trap
The Planet of Peril
The Star Pirates
The Claws of Christmas
The Sun-Snatchers
Revenge of the FANG
The Carnivore Curse
The Dreams of Dread

ASTROSAURS ACADEMY
DESTINATION: DANGER!
CONTEST CARNAGE!
TERROR UNDERGROUND!
JUNGLE HORROR!
DEADLY DRAMA!
CHRISTMAS CRISIS!

www.astrosaurs.co.uk

C.I.A

COWS IN ACTION

Aston!

THE VICTORIAN MOO-DERS

Steve Cole (signature)

Steve Cole

Illustrated by Woody Fox

RED FOX

THE VICTORIAN MOO-DERS
A RED FOX BOOK 978 1 862 30883 1

First published in Great Britain by Red Fox,
an imprint of Random House Children's Books
A Random House Group Company

This edition published 2010

1 3 5 7 9 10 8 6 4 2

Text copyright © Steve Cole, 2010
Illustrations by Woody Fox, copyright © Random House Children's Books, 2010

The right of Steve Cole to be identified as the author
of this work has been asserted in accordance with
the Copyright, Designs and Patents Act 1988.

The Random House Group Limited supports the Forest Stewardship
Council (FSC), the leading international forest certification organization.
All our titles that areprinted on Greenpeace-approved FSC-certified paper
carry the FSC logo. Our paper procurement policy can be found at
www.rbooks.co.uk/environment.

Red Fox Books are published by Random House Children's Books,
61–63 Uxbridge Road, London W5 5SA

www.kidsatrandomhouse.co.uk
www.rbooks.co.uk

Addresses for companies within The Random House Group Limited
can be found at: www.randomhouse.co.uk/offices.htm

THE RANDOM HOUSE GROUP
Limited Reg. No. 954009

A CIP catalogue record for this book is available
from the British Library.

Printed and bound in Great Britain by
CPI Bookmarque, Croydon CR0 4TD

For Peter Sharpe

★ THE C.I.A. FILES ★

Cows from the present –
Fighting in the past to protect the future . . .

In the year 2550, after thousands of years of being eaten and milked, cows finally live as equals with humans in their own country of Luckyburger. But a group of evil war-loving bulls – the Fed-up Bull Institute – is not satisfied.

Using time machines and deadly ter-moo-na-tor agents, the F.B.I. is trying to change Earth's history. These bulls plan to enslave all humans and put savage cows in charge of the planet. Their actions threaten to plunge all cowkind into cruel and cowardly chaos . . .

The C.I.A. was set up to stop them.

However, the best agents come not from 2550 – but from the present. From a time in the early 21st century, when the first clever cows began to appear. A time when a brainy bull named Angus McMoo invented the first time machine, little realizing he would soon become the F.B.I.'s number one enemy . . .

COWS OF COURAGE — TOP SECRET FILES

PROFESSOR ANGUS MCMOO

Security rating: Bravo Moo Zero

Stand-out features: Large white squares on coat, outstanding horns

Character: Scatterbrained, inventive, plucky and keen

Likes: Hot tea, history books, gadgets

Hates: Injustice, suffering, poor-quality tea bags

Ambition: To invent the electric sundial

LITTLE BO VINE

Security rating: For your cow pies only

Stand-out features: Luminous udder (colour varies)

Character: Tough, cheeky, ready-for-anything rebel

Likes: Fashion, chewing gum, self-defence classes

Hates: Bessie Barmer, the farmer's wife

Ambition: To run her own martial arts club for farmyard animals

PAT VINE

Security rating: Licence to fill (stomach with grass)

Stand-out features: Zigzags on coat

Character: Brave, loyal and practical

Likes: Solving problems, anything Professor McMoo does

Hates: Flies not easily swished by his tail

Ambition: To find a five-leaf clover — and to survive his dangerous missions!

Prof. McMoo's TIMELINE OF NOTABLE HISTORICAL EVENTS

13.7 billion years BC

BIG BANG - UNIVERSE BEGINS

(and first tea atoms created)

4.6 billion years BC

PLANET EARTH FORMS

(good job too)

23 million years BC

FIRST COWS APPEAR

(23 million is my lucky number!)

1700 BC

SHEN NUNG MAKES FIRST CUP OF TEA

(what a hero!)

7000 BC

FIRST CATTLE KEPT ON FARMS

(Not a great year for cows)

1901 AD

QUEEN VICTORIA DIES

(she was not a-moo-sed)

2550 BC

GREAT PYRAMID BUILT AT GIZA

(by an Egyptian geezer!)

31 BC ROMAN EMPIRE FOUNDED

(Roam-Moo empire founded by a cow but no one remembers that)

1509 AD HENRY VIII COMES TO THE THRONE

(and probably squashes it)

1620 AD ENGLISH PILGRIMS SETTLE IN AMERICA

(bringing with them the first cows to moo in an American accent)

1066 AD BATTLE OF HASTINGS

(but what about the Cattle of Hastings?)

1939 AD WORLD WAR TWO BEGINS

(or World War Moo as it is known to cows)

2007 AD I INVENT A TIME MACHINE!!!

2500 AD COW NATION OF LUCKYBURGER FOUNDED

(HOORAY!)

2550 AD COWS IN ACTION RECRUIT PROFESSOR McMOO, PAT AND BO

(and now the fun REALLY starts...)

(about time!)

1903 AD FIRST TEABAGS INVENTED

THE VICTORIAN
MOO-DERS

Chapter One

A VICTORIAN VENTURE

"Get a move on, you useless idiots!"
A screeching voice echoed round the
farmyard. "I could've built that tower
myself by now with boxing gloves on
both hands!"

In his nearby field, Pat
Vine, a young bullock,
put his hooves in his
ears. Bessie Barmer's
voice was as horrible
as the rest of her! She
looked like a cross
between a hippo,
a baboon and a
battleship in dungarees,

but in fact she was the farmer's wife.
Normally she passed time by shouting
at the animals, but today some burly
builders were getting an ear-bashing.

"How dare you want a tea break?
You've only been working for nine
hours!" She put her huge hands on her
even huger hips. "My Victorian ancestors
lived in a fine old mansion with a
marvellous view, and I want one too!"

"She wants *something*, all right," one builder muttered, picking up his tools. "No one talks to us like that," he told Bessie. "We're off!"

"Fine — I'll finish the tower myself!" Bessie looked scarlet with rage as the builders hurried back to their van. "And I'll make it twice as tall as you were going to. I'll be able to see for miles!"

"Uh-oh," Pat murmured to himself.

"That means she'll be able to look out over the whole farm."

Bessie glanced over in his direction. Pat quickly stood on all fours like a normal cow. If the bullying old biddy ever found out that he belonged to a special breed of cattle more intelligent than she was . . .

Just then, Pat's big sister, Little Bo Vine – another clever cow – came striding towards him on her hind legs, chomping on bubble gum. "Wotcher, bruv!" she said.

"Get down," Pat hissed at her. "Barmy Barmer's on the warpath again."

Bo yawned and blew a gum bubble the exact same shade of purple as her brightly painted udder. "When isn't she?"

"I'll do the job better than them anyway," Bessie muttered, stomping away as the builders drove off. "I've got loads of tools in the garage . . ."

"Actually, she hasn't." Bo grinned. "I borrowed them to use as weights for my daily workout behind the chicken coop!"

"You can forget your work-out once Bessie's built her stupid tower," said Pat. "She'll be able to spy on us all day long. We'll have to act normal the whole time!"

Bo frowned. "Perhaps I should biff her one?"

"That won't stop the tower getting built."

"But it would make me feel better!"

Pat sighed. He was very different from

his sister. While Bo enjoyed a punch-up, Pat preferred puzzle solving. Where Bo rushed blindly into danger like a mad cow, Pat planned ahead. But aside from their both being bright, they had one very important thing in common . . .

They were members of a top-secret squad of time-travelling cow commandos known as the C.I.A. – the Cows In Action!

Pat still couldn't quite believe it. As a calf, he had never expected to join up with a world-saving band of cows from five hundred years in the future. But when you shared a field with a daring, slightly overbearing, brave, bold, bright and a bit bigheaded genius-inventor bull named Professor Angus McMoo, anything was possible . . .

"Hey, you two! Come quickly!" Pat's heart leaped at the urgency in the deep, familiar voice behind them. He turned to find Professor McMoo – a stocky, sharp-horned, glasses-wearing figure with white squares patterning his reddy-brown hide – in the doorway of his shed. "The C.I.A. are sending an emergency signal from the future."

"Woo-hoo!" Bo was off in a flash, haring towards the professor with Pat close behind. "Action, here we come!"

McMoo ushered them impatiently into the cool and shady shed, where a strange frothing, bubbling noise could be heard.

"What sort of a signal is that?" Pat wondered.

"The evaporated-milk alert," McMoo explained. "It's like a red alert, only with added vitamin A and D and sixty per cent of the water taken out."

Bo held her purple udder protectively. "I prefer my milk the way it is, thank you very much."

"That's quite udder-standable." The professor kicked away a hay bale to reveal a large bronze lever. "Pat – do the honours, will you?"

Pat beamed. "You mean, pull that lever to transform this rickety old shed into a super-special *Time* Shed, ready to zip off through time on a new mission?"

"No, I mean put the kettle on so we can have a nice cuppa," McMoo told him with a grin. "*Then* pull that lever!"

In a blur, Pat switched on the kettle, chucked tea bags into three mugs and leaped onto the lever. At once, a rattling, clanking sound started up as the timely transformation of McMoo's most amazing invention got underway! A bank of controls, shaped like an enormous horseshoe, rose up from the muddy ground fizzing with strange energy. Power-cords and cables snaked into sight and planks in the wall swung round to reveal futuristic controls. A large computer screen glided down from the rafters.

Then Bo
yelped as
a large
cupboard,
crammed full
of costumes
from a
thousand
different times
and places, shot
up from a pile of
straw and banged into her bottom. She
went whizzing through the air and
grabbed hold of the screen – which now
showed the image of a black, burly bull.
It was Yak, the devoted Director of the
Cows In Action.

"I just got a bump on the bum," Bo
cried, dangling from the monitor. "But
it was worth it to see you up close,
Yakky-babes!"

Yak scowled. "As one of my agents
you should call me Director, young lady."

"Whoops!" Bo winked. "Sorry, Director Young-Lady."

Pat sighed. "I'll finish making the tea!"

"What's up, Yak?" asked McMoo, polishing his glasses. "Apart from Bo up on the computer screen, that is."

"Trouble is brewing in the year 1851," said Yak grimly.

"1851!" McMoo put his specs back on his nose and rubbed his hooves. "We're well into Victorian times by then – what a great year! Two moons discovered around Uranus! Napoleon the Third formed the second French Empire! The Great Exhibition opened in London!"

Bo let go of the screen and dropped down to the floor. "What was so *great* about it?"

"Everything!" McMoo declared. "Six million people came to see the latest inventions from all over the world. Everything from farm tools to false teeth, steam-engines to envelope-makers—"

"Calm down, Professor," Yak interrupted. "Like I said, we've got trouble. F.B.I. trouble."

"The Fed-up Bull Institute?" Bo scowled. The F.B.I. were criminal time-twisters, always trying to change history so that cruel cows would rule the planet. "Whatever they're up to, we can handle it."

"But let's handle this cup of tea first,"
said McMoo, as Pat passed him an
extra-strong brew. "Go on, Yak — what's
occurring?"

"Our spies here haven't found out
much," Yak admitted. "But it seems
the F.B.I.'s targets are a bunch of
brilliant botanists."

"*What*-a-nists?" Pat frowned as he
passed Bo her tea.

"Botany is the study of bottoms," said
Bo, rubbing her own backside ruefully.

"It's the study of *plants*," McMoo corrected her. "The Victorians were very big on it. Explorers travelled all over the world in search of rare plants to bring back home to study."
He drained his cup and smacked his lips. "They did a lot of work growing tea plants, as it happens ..."

"Yes, well, these botanists were all members of a gentlemen's club called the Green Thumb," Yak went on quickly. "And they've all met with a sinister fate ..."

"Why would the F.B.I. target plant experts?" Pat wondered.

"There's more," said Yak. "From what our spies have overheard, it seems that Queen Victoria herself might somehow be involved."

"Queen Victoria!" McMoo laughed

with delight. "Imagine meeting her!"

"You don't *have* to imagine it – just *go*! I'm beaming over the place-and-date details of your mission right now . . ." Yak leaned forward, his grim, hairy face filling the screen. "It's time to quit with the chit-chat, troops, and hit the past – *fast*!"

Chapter Two

GONE CLUBBING

The journey back through history seemed to take no time at all. Professor McMoo's trusty shed blazed purple as it landed in a quiet leafy corner of London parkland.

"Moo-vellous!" The professor checked his controls. "It's April 29th, 1851, and we're in Hyde Park – the site of the Great Exhibition. It's due to start the day after tomorrow!" A dreamy look stole into his eyes. "I hope we've solved this case before the grand royal opening What a spectacle! What a sight!"

"Remind me to set my alarm clock," said Bo with zero enthusiasm. The costume cupboard had just spat out a pile of clothes and she was staring at them suspiciously. "These outfits look rubbish."

"They're the height of Victorian fashion!" McMoo told her. "Quickly, let's get dressed. And don't forget your ringblenders!"

Pat picked up one of the shiny metal gadgets from the bank of controls and smiled. Ringblenders looked like ordinary nose rings but they were a billion times better. When worn through the nostrils they projected optical illusions that made cows look just like humans — and even translated cattle-speak into any language on the planet.

Bo shoved in her own ringblender, then struggled into several petticoats and a pink gown with a bell-shaped skirt. A white lacy bonnet finished off her disguise. "Gross!" she complained.

Pat put on checked trousers, a fancy waistcoat and a loose-fitting frock coat then checked his human reflection. "Very dashing," he decided.

Bo snorted. "It makes *me* want to go dashing to the toilet!"

"You'll have a job," McMoo told her. "The first on-street public toilets don't open till next February – and they're only for gents!" By now he was looking quite the gent himself in his tall top hat and dark brown suit. A black cravat was smartly tied

beneath the high collar of his starched white shirt. "Now, come on. Victorian London's waiting outside!"

Bo sniffed. "What's so great about Victorian stuff?"

McMoo stared at her, open-mouthed.

"Maybe we'd better ask the computer," said Pat hastily. "The Victorian file, please!"

Information appeared on the big screen.

++Victorian Era. ++Queen Victoria ruled Britain and its empire — about a quarter of the planet's population — for 64 years, from 1837 to 1901. ++During this time Britain became the wealthiest and most powerful country in the world. ++ Millions of people stopped working the land and started working machines as new-fangled factories sprung up. ++Thousands of miles of railways were built, allowing high-speed travel all over the country. ++Many world-changing new inventions appeared, including cameras, bicycles, steamships, electric light, postage stamps, radio, motorcars, underground railways and flushing toilets.

"There!" cried McMoo. "What do you think of that little lot?"

"Pardon?" Bo popped up from behind a hay bale.  "I was just getting a snack!" She held up some fleshy leaves. "Look, I found some of that nice twenty-sixth-century clover that Yak sent us the other day . . ."

With a groan, McMoo pointed to the shed doors. "You can eat it later. Now, moooove!"

The cows hurried out into a bright spring morning and found themselves in the shade of a large weeping willow. Looming over them was some kind of a gigantic greenhouse, stretching up into the sky. Workmen swarmed around its lower storeys.

"The Crystal Palace." McMoo strolled towards it happily, with Pat and Bo

beside him. "Made with 293,655 panes of glass! Ten storeys high and longer than five football pitches placed end to end."

"Um, what about those botanists the F.B.I. are after?" Pat asked, aware that the professor was easily distracted. "Where is this Green Thumb Club anyway?"

"According to Yak's data, it's on a posh street called Pall Mall," said McMoo, raising his top hat to a group of workmen.

"Then let's check it out!" cried Bo, hitching up her dress and racing through the park. Pat and McMoo hurried after her.

Bo made for a large white stone arch that led on to a wide, busy street. But as Pat looked around he saw that it was very different from the streets in his time. The tall grand buildings were similar – shops and houses and theatres – but a

thick smell of smoke and muck was in
the air. Dozens of horse-drawn carriages
and buses clopped and rattled over filthy
cobblestones. Old women sold soup and
hot potatoes from barrows, blocking the
pavement and shouting about low prices
in high voices. Men in tall hats and long
coats with enormous moustaches strode

26

briskly through the din. A boy in rags
swept a path through the dirt in the road
so that grand ladies carrying parasols
could cross cleanly, and was given a coin
for his trouble.

They walked on through the hubbub
and before long had reached a quieter,
swankier street. The carriages that

rattled along here were smarter, as were
their horses.

"Aha!" McMoo declared, peering at a
brass plate on the whitewashed wall of
a tall, imposing
house flanked
by marble
pillars. "The
Green Thumb
Club. We've
arrived!"

"And so has someone else," Bo
observed as a spotless black cab pulled
up beside the posh building and a tall,
bearded, bony old man dressed all in
black jumped out.

"Good day," he said politely. "I don't
recognize you – are you visitors to my
club?"

"*Your* club?" McMoo beamed. "What
a stroke of luck! I'm Professor Angus
McMoo, this is my nephew Pat, and
Bonnie, my niece. We're just visiting."

"Sir Lawrence Pwee, at your service." The man bowed stiffly. "Which club member have you come to see?"

McMoo lowered his voice. "We'd *really* like to see the ones who have disappeared."

Sir Lawrence frowned. "I have tried my best to keep this delicate matter a secret, sir. What do you know of it?"

"Not nearly enough," McMoo admitted. "Which is why we've come to investigate. So!" He started up the steps to the front door. "Pop inside, shall we?"

"Just a moment, if you please!" Sir Lawrence looked cross. "This is a private and exclusive club for botanists. No riff-raff – and definitely no ladies!"

Bo's face darkened. "What?" She marched up to the plant-expert and

29

reached into her pocket. "Maybe *this* will change your mind about letting me in." With a flourish she yanked out a piece of her twenty-sixth-century clover and dangled it in front of his startled face. "Ever seen anything like this before?"

Sir Lawrence was astounded. He took the plant with trembling fingers. "Where . . . where did you find this?"

Bo snatched back the peculiar plant. "I'll tell you once you've let us inside. Deal?"

"Yes! Anything. Just let me study that plant!" Sir Lawrence ushered them up the steps and unlocked the front door. But as he pulled it open, a small, red-haired man came rushing out and crashed into them in a wild, shivering panic.

"Let me pass!" the man cried. "I've got to get away. Away, I say!"

Sir Lawrence grabbed hold of him. "Seymour Bushes, pull yourself together!

Whatever has happened?"

Seymour's face was white with fear. "It's the cow," he whispered. "The Black Cow of Doom is coming to get me like she got all the others. Nothing can stop her. *Nothing!*"

Chapter Three

MOO-DER MOST FOUL

"'The Black Cow of Doom'?" Pat looked about in confusion. "There's a *cow* in here?"

"That's cow-razzzzy!" said Bo, hoping her ringblender hadn't stopped working.

"A *demon* cow!" wailed Seymour. "She left her card. It fell out of my copy of *The Times*!"

Bo prised open his fist to reveal a piece of thick paper. Beside a picture of a nasty-looking black cow was a note:

BEWARE, MR BUSHES! FOR I, THE DREADED BLACK COW OF DOOM, WILL SURELY MOO-DER YOU BEFORE THIS DAY IS OUT!

"Did the other disappearing botanists get a card like this?" asked McMoo.

"All of them," Sir Lawrence confirmed. "And sure enough, some time later a supernatural cow appeared to each in his home and snatched him away."

McMoo frowned. "People actually saw it?"

"Oh, yes," Sir Lawrence said gravely.

Pat gulped. "So is 'moo-der' the same as . . . murder?"

"I suppose so," said McMoo. "Only committed by a cow."

"Alas!" Seymour cried through chattering teeth. "I am doomed! Doomed to be dragged to the spirit world by a ghostly heifer!"

"Hush, Seymour, there is a lady present." Sir Lawrence turned to Bo, "I am so sorry you've had to hear such frightful words, my dear."

"I've heard worse, Larry," Bo assured him. "Words like 'pants', 'bums', 'drippy

33

poos', 'udder-rash'—"

Luckily before Sir Lawrence and Seymour could turn any paler another man came staggering through the hallway towards them. He was short and portly and looked quite unwell.

"Thank heaven you caught old Seymour," the man wheezed, holding one hand to his chest. "When he found that card, I was worried he might do himself a mischief – and that so might I, chasing after him!"

"Professor, Pat, Miss Bonnie, may I present Mr Dicky Hart." Sir Lawrence sighed. "Aside from Seymour, he's the club's only remaining member."

"I'm not surprised," said Bo. "Frankly, this club is a bit rubbish. You should buy a killer sound system and play more R&B."

Sir Lawrence, Seymour and Dicky stared at her blankly.

"But, er, getting back to this strange cow business that we've come to investigate," said Pat quickly. "Seymour, you said this card was in your copy of *The Times*. Where did that paper come from?"

"It's the club's copy," said Seymour.

Dicky clutched at his chest with renewed vigour. "I read it myself this morning, but found no card."

"Then someone must have put it there," McMoo declared. "We must speak to the servants and search the building."

"Must we indeed?" Sir Lawrence frowned at McMoo. "I say, sir, you are being rather high-handed."

"Better do as he says." Bo held up the

piece of twenty-sixth-
century clover and
waved it in front of
his nose. "It would
be a real shame if
this wilted before you
could study it . . ."

Sir Lawrence looked longingly at the
plant. "Oh, very well," he sighed. "Dicky,
take Seymour back to the drawing room
for a stiff drink would you? I'll gather
the servants together."

"Right you are," Dicky wheezed,
helping up Seymour. "This way. Slowly."

"And don't worry, Mr Bushes." Bo
flexed her muscles. "Any cow coming
after you will have to get through me
first!"

The C.I.A. agents swiftly searched the
grand old building from top to bottom.
Pat was usually very good at finding
things. But they could find no sign of

a break-in and not a single trace of a spooky cow.

Bo sat down crossly in an empty study. "Whoever left that scary card must have run straight outside again."

"But Sir Lawrence had to unlock the front door when we came in, remember?" Pat said. "They couldn't have got out that way."

"So they must have taken the tradesmen's entrance round the back," said McMoo. "Let's see if any of the servants spotted an intruder."

Pat, Bo and the professor trooped downstairs to the drawing room and pushed open the door. A small gaggle of footmen, butlers and kitchen staff stood smartly in front of Sir Lawrence. Seymour and Dicky were sitting nervously in armchairs. But the agents' eyes were riveted at once to a short, round woman, bulging out of a long black dress and a white lacy apron . . .

"I don't believe it!" Pat groaned. The woman looked just like Bessie Barmer! Bo gasped and pointed. "It's her, Sir Larry! Case closed. *She* did it!"

The Bessie-lookalike looked shocked. "Beg pardon, miss?"

"This is Eliza Barmer, my loyal housekeeper," said Sir Lawrence, outraged. "She has been in my employ for many years."

"I bet she did it anyway!" Bo cried.

"Shhh!" McMoo clamped a hoof over her mouth. "We can't accuse her just because of who she looks like."

Pat shook his head. "How come we always run into her ancestors whichever time we end up in?"

"Perhaps living so close to the Time Shed has left Bessie's DNA imprinted on the quantum-flux drive units," McMoo suggested, "resulting in a gene-generating time transfer to someone in the local population for every age we visit."

Bo went cross-eyed. "Eh?"

"Or maybe it's just bad luck!" McMoo turned back to Eliza and doffed his hat. "Forgive my niece's enthusiasm, miss."

"Beggin' your pardon, sir," a kitchen boy piped up. "Miss Barmer's been in the kitchen all morning."

A young maid nodded. "She's not been out of our sight, and we've not been out of hers."

"Everyone in the house has been accounted for," Sir Lawrence agreed.

"Then . . ." Eliza put her other hand

to her forehead. "That terrible card what Mr Bushes found really *was* delivered by a ghost!" With a feeble squeal she swooned and fell to the floor with a crash that shook the club to its foundations. Two footmen struggled to lift her onto a sofa and Sir Lawrence offered her smelling salts.

"Oh, dear." Seymour jumped up from his chair, wringing his hands. "I have to go. I really have to go at once!"

"No, Seymour," said Sir Lawrence. "You're in danger. You must not go anywhere alone at any time. Ever."

"Erm . . ." Seymour blushed. "I mean I have to *go* – to the lavatory!"

Eliza almost fainted again, and quickly jammed the smelling salts up her nose.

"I'll walk you there, Mr Bushes,"

McMoo offered. "Sir Lawrence is right —
you need protection at all times."

Seymour nodded gratefully and
led the way down a passage to some
French windows. They opened onto a
sunny courtyard crammed full of plants,
where a sort of tall wooden shed stood
at one end.

"Of course," McMoo muttered. "The
toilets were kept outside in Victorian
times."

"Shan't be a jif," said Seymour,
crossing the courtyard. But scant seconds
after he'd closed the door, he wailed
in surprise and alarm. "What? Miss
Barmer!" He started banging from inside
the toilet. "Oh, goodness!"

McMoo frowned. "What is it,
Seymour? What's wrong?"

His only reply was a spooky, wailing
groan as an eerie figure floated out
through the toilet door. Shudders ran
down the professor's spine. The figure

had huge, shadowy horns. Red eyes
glowed in its black face. A swollen,
sinister udder hung down from its body
like a set of bagpipes.

"So *you're* the Black Cow of Doom,"
breathed McMoo.

"MOOOO-DERRRRR!" hissed the
terrifying spirit-cow as it swirled towards
him . . .

Chapter Four

A RIGHT ROYAL VISIT

As the phantom reached out with its smoky hooves, Professor McMoo dived aside and landed painfully on a potted plant. A deafening, spooky-sounding *moo* echoed around the courtyard and the Black Cow swooped towards him again. Frantically McMoo rolled out of the way – but as he did so, he knocked his top hat against the wall so that the brim jammed down over his eyes.

"Mr Bushes!" the professor cried, tugging at his hat, unable to see. "Seymour! Are you all right?" At last the headwear came free, and he saw the sinister, shadowy cow growing larger and darker, whizzing around faster and faster in front of the outside toilet . . .

Then a throaty war-yell rang out. "Get out of it, ghost! It's time *YOU* were haunted – by my hooves of fury!" It was Little Bo – flying through the air in a kung-*moo* leap!

"No, Bo!" McMoo shouted. "Stay back!"

But it was too late. Bo went shooting straight *through* the whirling phantom figure and crashed into the outside loo.

The little hut broke apart with a splintering crash and Bo disappeared under a pile of planks. The ghostly visitor carried on whirling and whizzing about as if nothing had happened.

Pat, Sir Lawrence and Eliza Barmer appeared at the French windows, closely followed by Dicky Hart. "Upon my soul!" Sir Lawrence spluttered. Pat gasped, Dicky clutched his chest and Eliza swooned yet again.

Then, as suddenly as it had arrived, the phantom cow faded away to nothing.

Pat ran over to join the professor, who was already helping Bo up from the wreckage of the lav.

She groaned weakly. "Did I get it?"

"If you mean a sore head, then the answer's yes." McMoo sighed. "If you mean the Black Cow of Doom, then I'm afraid not. Good try, though!"

"Was it really a spirit, Professor?" Pat

wondered, his eyes wide.

McMoo kicked about in the scattered planks. "Well, it's certainly *spirited* away poor old Seymour!"

"Mr Bushes has been moo-dered!" wailed Eliza Barmer from the mossy courtyard floor.

With some effort, McMoo helped her up. "When Seymour saw whatever he saw in the toilet, he shouted for you, Mrs Barmer. Any idea why?"

Eliza sobbed into a hanky. "None, sir! None!"

"Probably hoped she might scare the ghost away!" Bo muttered.

Then Pat noticed something glinting on the ground beside the wreck of the toilet. "Hey!" He picked up a large silver and ivory brooch. "What's this?"

"Ooh! That's mine!" Eliza dried her eyes and took the brooch from him. "How peculiar. I thought I had left it in my quarters."

"Perhaps Seymour spotted it and called to let you know," said Sir Lawrence. "But then that foul farmyard fiend appeared and . . ."

"We'll see Seymour no more!" Dicky wiped a tear from his eye. "And I fear that I shall be the cow's next target."

"*Not so, sir!*" came a shrill, regal voice from behind them.

Everyone whirled round, and gasped.

McMoo couldn't believe his eyes! A short, dumpy woman had spoken. She looked sullen and grave, with bulging eyes. Her long, dark hair was pinned back behind her ears with not a strand out of place; her blue satin dress hung down to her feet just as faultlessly. There was a haughty look about her that spoke of someone used to getting their own way. Beside her stood a slender man with a small, neat moustache. He looked from person to person, nodding his head politely.

Sir Lawrence gasped and fell quickly to one knee, as did the other humans – apart from Eliza who simply fell to the floor. "Your Majesty!" Sir Lawrence spluttered.

"And His Royal Highness, the Prince Consort!" cried McMoo in delight. He quickly put an arm around Pat and Bo and shoved them to their knees. "Queen Victoria herself turning up with her

hubby," he whispered, "and we're here to see it. I *love* this job!"

"Er, forgive me, ma'am," stammered Sir Lawrence. "And you, dear Albert, my old friend. I'm sorry for not greeting you when first you arrived here, but I was not expecting a royal visit."

"Naturally, you weren't," said Queen Victoria, a girlish sparkle in her eyes. "Because we are here in secret! We came in an unmarked carriage."

McMoo was looking between Sir Lawrence and Albert. "Are you two mates, then? I didn't know you were a botanist, your prince-ness."

"It's one of my hobbies," Albert explained in his German accent. "And Sir Lawrence and his friends have helped me a great deal with preparations for the Great Exhibition by creating the many plant displays." He shook his head. "I was so shocked when Sir Lawrence told me about the Black Cow's moo-derous antics . . ."

"And now," said Victoria, "it seems that the vile, moo-dering phantom wants to get my dear husband! Infernal cheek. Show them, Albert."

Albert removed a by now familiar card from his jacket pocket. "This was

delivered to my table
at my private club." Sir
Lawrence and Dicky Hart
crowded round to read,
and McMoo, Pat and Bo
looked over their shoulders.

BEWARE, ALBERT! screamed the printed
words. *I, THE DREADED BLACK COW OF
DOOM, WILL MOO-DER YOU. DON'T EVEN
THINK OF TRYING TO FIND A PROTECTIVE
CHARM IN AN OLD BOOK OF MAGIC FROM
YOUR LOCAL ANTIQUE BOOK STORE — IT
WILL AVAIL YOU NAUGHT!*

"You see now why we came here in
secret," said Albert. "If the newspaper
men knew I had been threatened
by a ghostly cow, and that I took it
seriously—"

"The royal family would look
ridiculous," huffed Queen Victoria. "It
wouldn't do for all those foreigners
visiting the exhibition to think we're
scaredy-cats!"

"The Black Cow was in a chatty mood when it wrote this card," Pat observed. "Seymour's note was short and not very sweet."

"The cow was foolish to even mention that charm," said Queen Victoria. "I sent an advisor straight out to the nearest antique bookshop in Piccadilly. And sure enough, he found a most telling piece of parchment with ease!" She pulled out a crumpled roll of paper from the sleeve of her dress, and read aloud: "*To ward off the fearsome spirit of the Black Cow of Doom, you must go to a house with three marble fountains and a garden where grows the pomp lily.*"

Sir Lawrence looked amazed. "But . . . my own house has three fountains! And the pomp lily grows in my garden in abundance!"

"I know, my friend, from past visits." Albert smiled. "And the Black Cow must have known also, which is why it tried to steer me away from learning of such a charm."

"But instead, it accidentally gave you the idea," McMoo noted thoughtfully. "What a careless ghost."

"Quite!" Victoria agreed, turning to Sir Lawrence. "But since we wish to take no chances with the Great Exhibition's grand opening ceremony in just forty-eight hours, I wondered if Albert and I could secretly stay with you until that time?"

"Majesty, of course! It would be an honour!" Sir Lawrence bowed low enough to kiss the ground, as Albert smiled his thanks. "And Dicky, you must come too," he told his friend. "We know now that the Black Cow can strike here in my club – it may try to get you too while we're away."

"A right royal stay in the country?" Dicky went red with delight. "Goodness me, the old ticker won't stand it!"

"Er, might I see that parchment, Your Majesty?" McMoo gave her a winning smile. "I'm Professor Angus McMoo, by the hay. *Way*, I mean. Expert on everything cow-ish."

Victoria passed him the paper with a girlish smile. "I hope *you* will be joining us also, Professor? I do so admire men of learning."

"Ha!" Bo whispered. "Queen Victoria fancies you!"

"Well, *I* certainly fancy a trip to Sir Lawrence's." McMoo held the parchment to his lips, took a sneaky lick and nodded. "As I thought, this is a fake. It's just modern paper stained with tea to make it look yellowy and old." He tasted the parchment again. "And not just any old tea. Unless my taste buds are very much moo-staken, it's a blend from the twenty-sixth century!"

"Then . . . this was left in the queen's local antique book shop on purpose for her to find." Pat gasped. "Those Fed-up Bulls must *want* Albert and Dicky to go to Sir Lawrence's house."

Bo scratched her head. "But why? If Albert isn't even a real botanist . . ." She gasped suddenly. "Hey! Yak told us that Queen Vicki might be part of the  F.B.I. plan – do you think those fed-up bulls are trying to get at her?"

"Quite possibly," McMoo agreed.

Bo frowned. "Then we must warn her and Albert!"

"Warn them about time-travelling bulls from the future? They'd never believe us." The professor shook his head. "No, our best bet is to stay close, learn what the F.B.I. are up to and do our best to protect everyone."

Pat swallowed hard. "What if our best isn't good enough?"

"It'll have to be," McMoo declared. "Whatever the risks or the dangers we face – the F.B.I.'s time-crime must be stopped!"

Chapter Five

TRAIN OF DANGER

Within the hour, two more horse-drawn carriages had pulled up outside the Green Thumb Club. McMoo, Pat and Bo eagerly jumped into the first and Eliza Barmer staggered down the steps into

the second, helped by two of Sir
Lawrence's footmen. She had packed
two giant suitcases, one green and one
yellow, each almost as big as she was.
The carriage groaned as she heaved
them on board.

"What's she got in there?" Bo
wondered. "Can't be beauty products!"

"Don't be mean," said Pat. "She seems
quite nice for a Barmer."

The queen and Prince Albert led Sir
Lawrence and Dicky Hart down to their
unmarked horse and carriage. Once
they'd climbed aboard, their driver set

off, leading the procession of coaches to Euston station.

McMoo leaned out of the window as they rattled along, enjoying the sights and sounds and smells of the bustling Victorian  streets. Bo, on the other hand, sat holding her nose from the stink of oil and smoke and sewage.

"Professor, what if the ghost of the Black Cow attacks Prince Albert on the way to Sir Lawrence's house?" asked Pat.

"Bud der F.B.I. don't dow wad drain dey'll be gedding," said Bo still holding her nose.

"The F.B.I. might know very well which train they'll be getting," McMoo pointed out, "if Sir Lawrence Pwee is working for them!"

"Pulsating parsnips!" Pat gasped. "I suppose it is a bit strange that the victims so far all belonged to his club – and that only his house can keep the ghost away."

Bo let go of her nose. "It could also explain why he's got a rotten old Barmer as his housekeeper. But he seems such a nice geezer!"

"We'll keep an eye on him *and* Eliza," said McMoo. "And guard Vicki and Albert especially closely." Their carriage pulled up outside what appeared to be a massive, old-fashioned temple. "Aha! Here we are, the way into Euston station. Time for a real-life Victorian railway experience!"

While Dicky hurried off to buy tickets, Sir Lawrence escorted Victoria and Albert into the station's grand hall – a gigantic space lined with archways, offices and galleries, with a

high, ornate ceiling. McMoo, Pat and
Bo hurried after them, followed by
Eliza and the footmen who wheeled
the luggage on funny wooden trolleys.

The royals wore big hats and long black
cloaks to disguise themselves, and though
the hall was teeming with people no one
spared them a glance as Sir Lawrence
led the way to a shining green steam
engine. It stood beside the platform,
spitting steam and smoke.

McMoo beamed at Sir Lawrence as
the footmen heaved the bags and boxes
into the train's luggage compartment.
"So, who's sitting where? Bagsy I ride
with my back to the engine!"

"As a gentleman, McMoo, I'm sure you're aware that a first-class coach seats four people on each side," said Sir Lawrence. "Therefore, to make sure we have privacy, you and your young companions may join Dicky and I in sitting with Her Majesty and Prince Albert." He looked at Eliza. "Mrs Barmer, while my footmen travel in second class, I will let you take the remaining seat to be sure a stranger does not join us."

Eliza gasped. "Why, thank you, sir!"

"Travelling with other people's servants!" The short queen gave a regal sigh. "If the Prime Minister could see me now!" She took Albert's hand and climbed up into the carriage. Dicky and Sir Lawrence followed and the C.I.A. agents pushed on board after them.

The first-class compartment was made of polished wood and had thickly padded seats, carpet on the floor and shutters on the windows. Eliza gasped in wonder. Then a loud whistle sounded from the platform. With a hissing noise, the mighty locomotive pulled away from the station. It picked up speed, chuffing and rattling and bumping along.

McMoo looked as happy as a pig in mud as the towers and chimneys of town slowly gave way to green countryside. Eliza cooed quietly, her fingers playing with the brooch on her coat.

"That's a very pretty little thing,"

Queen Victoria remarked. "For a servant to wear, I mean. May I see it?"

"Er . . ." Eliza blushed scarlet. "Of course, ma'am." She carefully removed it and passed it over. "Sir Lawrence gave it to me."

"Merely a bauble," said Sir Lawrence quickly. "To celebrate Mrs Barmer passing twenty years in my employment."

Bo whispered to Pat: "Someone should give him a medal for sticking with the old bat for so long!"

"That was a fine evening." Dicky Hart turned fondly to Eliza. "Remember what you cooked for us at the club that night, my dear?"

"Um . . ." Eliza shrugged. "Parsnip stew?"

Dicky frowned. "It was clear turtle

soup followed by roast goose with all the trimmings!"

"Oh, yes! Sorry, sir." She meekly accepted the brooch back from Queen Victoria. "I'm afraid I'm not feeling quite myself. This dreadful cow business . . ."

As if on cue, a ghostly, all too familiar wailing started up over the frantic chuffing of the engine.

"Uh-oh," said McMoo as a dark, shadowy figure with glowing red eyes and two trembling horns swam into sight in the middle of the coach.

"The Black Cow!" yelled Dicky as Albert and Sir Lawrence cowered in fear.

"What? Oh, my!" Eliza dropped the brooch in fright. "It will moo-der us all!"

"Back again, huh?" Bo struck a fighting pose as the ghost began to swirl about the compartment, roaring and hissing. "Well, you won't get away from me *this* time!" She lunged towards the ghostly cow but again she went

right through
it, this time
accidentally
punching
Pat! He
sank back
in his chair
in a daze.

"That vile
phantom must
be after my lovely
Albert!" Victoria cried. "It knows we
are on our way to safety, and seeks to
strike first. Don't let it get him – that's a
royal command!"

"Then there's only one place to
go," said McMoo. He charged straight
through the ghost, yanked Albert to his
feet and threw open the carriage door!
A smoky, sooty gale rushed in as
McMoo dragged the alarmed Prince
outside, balancing on the footboards
and clinging to the windowsill.

"This is madness, Professor!" spluttered
Albert.

"Nah. Bit of fresh air, lovely!" McMoo
cried. "Ghostly cows can really fog
up a carriage." Even as he spoke, the
phantom of the Black Cow followed,
spiralling out through the door, reaching
for them with dark, shadowy hooves.
Albert whimpered with fear, but McMoo
edged away along the footboard, pulling
the prince after him.

"Help!" Albert shouted, keeping a tight

grip on the windowsill. "If the Black Cow doesn't get me, you most surely will!"

"I just want to know if that ghost is for real, or just some sort of parlour trick," McMoo explained. Suit flapping in the gale, he leaped across and perched precariously on the footboards of the neighbouring carriage. "If it *is* real, it should be able to follow us wherever we go."

Albert gulped as he wriggled across to the next coach too, pressing himself flat against the woodwork. "Follow us and moo-der us?"

"Probably," McMoo agreed cheerily.

By now, Bo, Pat and Queen Victoria were leaning out through the door of their carriage – Bo swiped uselessly at the still-hovering ghost with her hooves and the queen shook a royal fist. "Save my husband, Professor!" she hollered. "Or I will *NOT* be amused!"

"Oh, no!" Pat cried. "Here comes a tunnel!"

With a stab of fear, McMoo saw Pat was right. The train was plunging towards a deep black hole in the hillside up ahead. And while the Black Cow was making no attempt to chase after Albert, he supposed it hardly needed to. "If we're still holding on outside when the train enters the tunnel," he muttered, "we'll be scraped across the walls like strawberry jam!"

Chapter Six

COWNTRY HOUSE

Clinging on by the tips of his hooves, McMoo watched helplessly as the train thundered ever closer towards the beckoning blackness of the tunnel. He and Albert had maybe thirty seconds before it roared inside.

With red eyes glowing and its ghostly udder trembling, the Black Cow started spinning in the air faster and faster outside Sir Lawrence's carriage, roaring as though laughing its horns off.

And then suddenly it vanished.

"Ha!" shouted Bo, as Sir Lawrence appeared at the window with Eliza just behind him. "I scared it away!"

"The phantom simply knows its work is done, foolish child," moaned Albert. "It has doomed me!"

"We're not doomed yet!" McMoo yelled back, his mind racing. Could he and Albert jump for it? No, the hillside behind them was steep and littered with sharp rocks – if  they struck one at this speed . . .

Suddenly, the sound of screams carried from inside the carriage McMoo and Albert now clung on to, as a gaggle of terrified old ladies caught sight of their two unexpected visitors. Albert started wailing too, rigid with fear as the speeding train tore ever closer to the tunnel. With only seconds to go, the professor knew he could never manhandle the panicking prince through the door in time . . .

So he lowered his horns and smashed his head through the carriage window!

The ladies screeched louder. Albert joined in with their discordant cries. Then, fighting against the gusting wind, McMoo grabbed Albert and propelled him through the hole in the glass with a power-packed punt up the princely posterior . . . delivering him safely into the old ladies' carriage!

"Hurrah!" Queen Victoria cheered from the other compartment.

"*Moooo-ve* it, Professor!" Bo bellowed.

The tunnel's dark and smoky mouth
seemed to widen, ready to swallow the
speeding locomotive – and to squash
the unusual passenger holding on
outside. The driver sounded the whistle.

Desperately, McMoo
struggled to
squeeze his bullish
bulk through
the carriage
window . . . and
tumbled inside
just as the
train burst into
the tunnel. The
professor shut his eyes
as deafening echoes and thick sooty
smoke blew in through the broken
window for half a minute or more.
Finally, he opened his eyes to find the
train had passed right through the tunnel
and was back in the sunlight, chuffing
serenely on its way. Prince Albert was

sitting in a daze beside him, while four white-faced old ladies peered down at them anxiously.

"Sorry to drop in on you like this." McMoo scrambled to his feet and grinned. "Don't suppose there's any chance of a cup of tea . . . ?"

The professor didn't get any tea, but he *did* get some fruitcake and sympathy once the ladies accepted his story that Albert had sleepwalked out of his carriage and McMoo was trying to save his life. Luckily, they didn't recognize Albert as the husband of the British queen. "Good job there's no Victorian version of *Hello!* magazine," McMoo noted.

In another few minutes, the train stopped at a station and McMoo and Albert staggered unsteadily outside.

"You saved my Albert!" Queen Victoria ran out onto the platform and

embraced her husband. Then she flung
her chubby arms around the professor
too. "I shall make you a knight."

"Been there, done that." McMoo
grinned cheekily. "I'd sooner you made
me a majestic cuppa . . . !" But
Victoria had already turned away,
leading Albert back to their carriage.

While Dicky and Eliza took a brisk
stroll to calm their nerves and Sir
Lawrence tried to clear up the matter
of the broken carriage window with the
station master, the C.I.A. agents conferred

on the platform. "I thought you were both goners for sure, out there," said Pat. "That Black Cow ghost is horrible."

"I don't believe it *is* a real ghost," McMoo revealed. "Tunnel or no tunnel, it couldn't follow Albert to the next carriage."

"Then what is it?" asked Bo.

"I don't know," McMoo admitted.

"Well, I'm going to search the train for F.B.I. agents," Bo declared, marching off down the platform.

Pat and the professor went with her. But there was no sign of anyone remotely suspicious on the train.

"If the F.B.I. *are* around," said Pat, "they're staying well-hidden."

McMoo nodded moodily. "But sooner or later, when we least expect it . . . they'll strike!"

The rest of the journey to Sir Lawrence's passed quietly. As the train approached

Commoner's Halt, the last station on the line, eight sighs of relief filled the first-class compartment.

Hidden once more beneath hats and cloaks, Victoria and Albert followed Sir Lawrence and Dicky to where cab drivers stood waiting beside their coaches and horses. Eliza helped the

footmen load the luggage onto a second coach, and the C.I.A. agents hopped into a third. The horses pulled away and the intrepid gang braced themselves for the final leg of their journey.

"That train was slower than a hedgehog with one foot," Bo complained. "This investigation's going nowhere!"

"I think you'll find it's going to a very big house in the country," McMoo corrected her. "And everyone's come here because that faked parchment said a house with three fountains and pomp lilies will give protection from the Black Cow," said McMoo. "But what if the *reverse* is true?"

"You mean, *Cow Black the from protection gives lilies pomp and fountains three with house A*?" Bo joked. "Doubt it."

McMoo pulled a face. "I mean, those lilies and fountains could be part of an evil F.B.I. plan to make the Black Cow stronger and more dangerous, somehow. We must check them out as soon as we can!"

Before long, Sir Lawrence's fine country house came into sight – a grand, towering slab of stone and ivy.

The impressive grounds were crammed
with a thousand different plants, all in
full bloom.

Pat pointed. "There are the fountains!"

Three circular pools stood in a neatly
mown lawn. A huge stone trout, spitting
water from its mouth, balanced in each.

"Let's hope that's the only fishy thing
about these fountains," said McMoo.
"Bo, check them out – carefully – and
stand guard by them till we join you."

"Gotcha, Prof," cried Bo. She leaped

from the moving carriage and hurried
away.

"As for you, Pat, I'd like you to
search Sir Lawrence's house from top
to bottom," McMoo said. "But do it
sneakily. If there is an F.B.I. agent here,
our best hope is to catch them
off guard."

"I'll do my best," Pat promised. "What
are you going to do?"

The professor smiled. "I'm going
to find out if a pomp lily a day keeps

black cows away!"

As their carriage arrived outside the house, McMoo and Pat jumped down to join the others.

"One is tired," Queen Victoria announced. "One is going to bed."

Pat stretched. "I'd like a lie down too, please."

"Of course," said Sir Lawrence. "Mrs Barmer, kindly escort Her Majesty to the main bedroom, and Pat to one of the guest chambers."

Eliza curtseyed. Then she noticed one of the footmen struggling to shift her two enormous cases, and she rushed over to help.  "May I lie down as well after that, sir? I am feeling quite under the weather."

"Very well," Sir Lawrence answered.

"I say, McMoo," Dicky said, watching as Eliza plodded off with her luggage, the queen and Pat in tow. "Where's your niece?"

"Oh, just taking a stroll in the grounds," McMoo told him airily. "She does like a bit of nature. Speaking of which, Sir Lawrence, I'd love to see one of your pomp lilies . . ."

"As would I," said Albert. "I want to be sure they are still here to protect us!"

"Then let us go at once," declared Sir Lawrence. "Come along!"

Over by the fountains, Bo was getting bored. She'd checked out the trouts, tasted the water and even had a quick paddle. But there seemed nothing remotely trap-like about them.

Then suddenly, Bo heard a rustle from the bushes ahead of her. A wisp of steam rose up from their depths. "Professor?" she called.

A top hat peeped out from the vegetation, then vanished back inside with a choking cry.

"Prof!" Bo charged towards the bushes, hooves raised. "Hang on. I'll save you!" She leaped headfirst into the greenery ...

And straight into a cast-iron hoof. *CLANG!*

"Oof!" Bo cried, collapsing in a leafy tangle. She  caught a blurred glimpse of a broad metal face staring down at her with glowing green eyes ...

"A ter-moo-nator!" she breathed. "Got to warn the others ..."

"It is too late, my dear," hissed a scary, metallic voice as blackness overwhelmed her. "*Far* too late ..."

Chapter Seven

THE TRAP IS SPRUNG

From the window of a luxurious guest room in the sprawling mansion, Pat watched Professor McMoo vanish into the leafy gardens with Sir Lawrence, Prince Albert and Dicky Hart. Beyond a row of fir trees he could see the fishy tips of the three fountains – but no sign of Bo.

"She'll be OK," he told himself. "Probably just off clobbering something." He crossed to the door and peeped out onto the deserted landing. "I hope the queen's a heavy sleeper . . ."

It was time to start searching the house.

Pat started by checking several rooms along the landing. Then he quickly hid as the footmen came up to do some dusting.

"This is Eliza's job," he heard one grumble.

"I quite like it!" said the other happily. "Besides, it's plain to see that poor dear Eliza is really worn out ..."

Pat decided that this would be a good time to search the servants' quarters. He crept down a large curving staircase and started sticking his snout into the poky, musty rooms below stairs where Sir Lawrence's servants had to live.

Suddenly, he heard a strange, muffled moaning sound coming from behind a heavy wooden door. "Mff-phhh-rrrph!" Nervously, he moved closer and turned the handle.

The moaning grew more urgent. "Mrphhh-mmph!"

Pat went inside. From the giant

bloomers hanging by the window, he
knew this must be Eliza's room. Then
he saw one of her oversized suitcases
– the green one – on the narrow bed.
It was rocking – and the moaning and
groaning was coming from inside!

Heart pounding, hooves trembling,
Pat undid the clasps and the lid flew
open . . . To reveal Eliza Barmer – trussed
up and helpless inside her own trunk,
gagged with a long woolly stocking!
Pat quickly pulled away the gag.
"Help me!" cried Eliza, her eyes wide
and fearful.

"Mrs Barmer!" Pat frowned. "Who tied you up and stuffed you in there?"

"I did!" came a gruff voice from behind him.

Pat whirled round – just in time to see the frying pan zooming towards his head. A split  second later, it struck – and all he saw were stars, fading quickly into darkness . . .

McMoo paced impatiently round a large pond while Sir Lawrence showed off his pomp lilies to Prince Albert and Dicky. There seemed nothing unusual about them – no tripwires to trigger traps, no poisonous thorns, no deadly squirters hidden inside the delicate white flowers . . .

"Of course, these plants may well become extinct within years," lectured Sir Lawrence. "They are extremely rare."

"And getting rarer, old chap," said Dicky, peering at a large patch of dug-up earth beside the pond. "Didn't you have another big clump of them growing just here?"

"Gracious!" Sir Lawrence stared at the spot in alarm. "Someone's pinched them!"

Albert turned pale. "Do you think there are enough lilies left to make sure we are all protected?"

But Sir Lawrence didn't reply – turning from the pond he had noticed something else. "My beautiful lawn! The grass has been chewed and chomped."

Suddenly, a piercing shriek rang out in the peaceful garden.

Dicky clutched his chest. "That sounds like Mrs Barmer! I thought she was resting."

"The shout came from behind those trees," McMoo pointed. "Come on!" He led the charge of Victorian gentlemen (although in Dicky's case it was more of a wobbly stagger) through to the other side of the little copse. But once there he skidded to a startled stop.

There was Eliza Barmer, clinging on to both her overstuffed suitcases and wailing for help.

"What's wrong?" puffed Sir Lawrence. "Why all the shouting?"

"And why bring your luggage out here?" Albert frowned.

"You won't believe what's happened to me!" shrieked Eliza.

"You might be right," McMoo agreed, staring past her. "Because I certainly don't believe *that*!"

Dicky Hart appeared beside him, and yowled in fear. "It's the Black Cow!"

A large beast was wandering out of a nearby rhubarb patch. It *looked* like the Black Cow at first glance – it was black, for a start, and maybe twice the size of ordinary cattle. But *this* black cow seemed solid and real.

"It is a ghost no longer!" Prince Albert gulped. "It is here in the fearsome flesh!"

"Fearsome's a bit too strong a word," McMoo muttered. "It looks a bit lost."

"But what about the fountains and the pomp lilies?" cried Dicky as the black cow wandered out of sight behind some bushes. "The parchment said they would keep that ghostly brute away!"

"It only said they would ward off the *spirit* of the cow," Eliza reminded him.

Albert nodded. "Perhaps that is why the ghost has turned itself into a thing of form and substance."

"We must go after it," cried Sir Lawrence. "That big cow must be made to pay!"

"I . . . I suppose it must." Dicky gulped. "Oh, my poor ticker!"

McMoo and the gentlemen set off in pursuit, Eliza wobbling along behind them with her suitcases. As they reached the bushes, they saw the black cow heading towards a large, ramshackle stable block, mooing as it went.

"It's been years since I kept horses there," panted Sir Lawrence. "But if the walls are still solid, perhaps we can trap it inside?"

"It's making things easy for us," McMoo noted as the Black Cow stalked into the stable block. "Something strange is going on here . . ."

"Come on, fellows!" said Sir Lawrence, picking up a big stick. "We must attack the cow!"

"Yes! I've run far enough." Albert clapped Dicky on the back. "Come on, man, we'll show that rotten Black Cow what British men are made of!"

"But you're German," McMoo reminded him.

"Don't be cheeky," Albert retorted.

"Well, I'll fight till I drop," Dicky declared, loosening his sweaty collar. "Although actually, that might not be long in coming."

"No, wait, all of you!" McMoo protested, hurrying after the determined men. "Something sneaky is going on. Someone *wants* you to go rushing after that thing without thinking . . ."

Sir Lawrence ignored him, lingering in the entrance to the stables with his allies. "The light is damnably dim in here."

"Not as dim as you lot!" cried Eliza Barmer — and with a thrust of her billowing belly she knocked Albert, Sir Lawrence, Dicky and McMoo sprawling to the dirty floor.

The next moment, bright lights snapped on in the rafters — *electric* lights, McMoo realized. The large cow was revealed at the back of the stable, munching calmly on hay. Then a frightening figure stepped out from behind it.

It was a ter-moo-nator, half-bull, half-machine — but like no ter-moo-nator McMoo had ever seen before. Iron-plates held together with rivets covered half its head and body. Its horns were like towering chimneys. Its chest was a barrel-shaped furnace, and its legs were like mighty pistons. Steam hissed from its metal snout.

"I am T-1901," said the ter-moo-nator, drawing a ray gun from a holster at its hip. "A master of illusion — and soon, master of the Victorian world!"

Chapter Eight

TWIN TROUBLES

"Save the boastful bull for someone who believes it, T-1901," said McMoo. "Whatever you're planning, it will never succeed."

"You can't stop me, Professor." The ter-moo-nator smiled, seeing straight through the ringblender's disguise. "Not while I hold your young friends Bo and Pat as my prisoners."

McMoo scowled. "Where are they?"

"Unharmed for now, tied up in the room next door." The ter-moo-nator stepped forward, a menacing smile on its lips. "They are far too dangerous to be allowed to roam freely, even though I do not need them – not in the way I need all of *YOU* . . ."

"What *is* that thing?" whispered Dicky.

Albert shrugged. "Where did it find that cow? And how does it know you, Professor?"

"I've met the likes of him in, er, *past* investigations," McMoo said carefully. "He's an enemy not only of Great Britain, but of the world. As for where he found the cow, I have no idea."

T-1901 smiled. "You will understand all, soon enough."

"I've *had* enough." Sir Lawrence raised a bony fist. "You, sir, are trespassing on my land. Be off with you!"

"I think you mean *beef* off with me," chuckled T-1901. "But *you* are the one who went away to stay at your club for a month – allowing me to set up a secret base in your grounds."

"With the help of Mrs Barmer, I presume," said Albert, glaring at Eliza. "How could you repay your master's kindness like this?"

"Easy," the big woman growled. "Because I'm *not* Eliza. I'm her twin sister – Fanny Barmer." With that, she set down the green suitcase and opened the lid – revealing poor Eliza trussed up and helpless inside.

"Twins!" squeaked Dicky. "Good lord, you're identical!"

"Except Eliza is a sick-making

goodie-goodie and I'm not," Fanny
snarled. "She would never agree to help
a talking, part-metal bull carry out his
evil plans in exchange for cash – unlike
me!"

"Of course," McMoo realized. "When
Seymour Bushes went to the outside
toilet he shouted Eliza's name because
he thought *you* were her. You were
hiding inside!"

She nodded proudly. "I went there as
soon as I'd sneaked in and slipped the
moo-der card in his paper – after a scare

like that, I knew he'd need the lav sooner
rather than later!"

"Mrrph-nnnnnn," Eliza said, speaking
forlornly through her gag.

"But whatever did you do with poor
Seymour?" demanded Dicky.

Fanny grimaced. "I've been carrying
him round with me ever since!" She
opened the yellow
case and Seymour
Bushes came
tumbling out,
bound and
gagged and
apparently
fast asleep.

"You fiendish
madam!" Sir Lawrence cried, checking
his chum was OK.

"The old boy fainted," said Fanny. "I
smuggled him out of the toilet while the
ghost-cow distracted the professor. Then
I hid in Eliza's room until she came to

pack, jumped her and took her place."

"Clever," McMoo admitted. "Rotten and horrible, but clever. I thought that so-called ghost had transported Seymour away. But it *was* just special effects, wasn't it? Some sort of laser projection . . . "

T-1901 smiled and nodded. "Projected by a device hidden inside Eliza's brooch."

Fanny glowered down at her sister. "I've had my eye on it for ages, ever since Sir Larry gave it to you."

"Curse you!" said Sir Lawrence. "You are both heartily wicked."

"True," T-1901 agreed. "But you will admit, gentlemen, that the Black Cow was a most effective terror weapon. It scared you all into making foolish decisions, such as rushing back here. And *you* were the biggest fool of all, my dear Albert!" He turned to the prince. "You thought you were being so clever, defying the Black Cow's calling card.

But *I* was the clever one, hiding the fake parchment in your local book shop."

"And all the time the Black Cow was simply an illusion!" Albert groaned. "But why set it off on the train? We were already coming to Sir Lawrence's house."

T-1901 frowned at Fanny. "Well, human?"

She blushed. "Stupid thing went off in my hand as I was showing it to the queen! It's not my fault I've got big fingers . . ."

"Never mind all that!" Sir Lawrence looked nervously at the metal monster. "Tell me, bull. Our fellow botanists who fell foul of your phantasmagoria . . . are *they* still alive, like Seymour?"

"They are my prisoners too," T-1901 confirmed, "working on a special project. At first, I thought I would only need one or two top botanists. But progress has been slow."

"So you had to 'moo-der' more and

more," Pat realized.

T-1901 nodded. "Now the entire club is here, the work will go much faster."

"We will never help you, sir!" squeaked Dicky.

"Just what are you up to, anyway?" demanded McMoo.

Wisps of steam escaped the ter-moo-nator's chimney-like horns as he pressed a button on his chest. "Observe!"

The back wall of the stable swung open on huge, invisible hinges — to reveal

a strange and sinister hidden room that seemed to be part-laboratory, part-garden centre. In the glare of artificial sunlight, exhausted-looking men in crumpled clothes were slaving away over curious experiments. Bits of leaf, twig and root lay all about, with weird-looking plants trailing out of test tubes or blossoming in bubbling beakers.

With a surge of relief, McMoo saw that Pat and Bo had not been harmed, although they were tied up tightly in a tangled heap around a thick wooden beam.

"Professor!" Bo cried.

"Help us, please!" begged Pat. "I've had Bo's bum in my face for ages."

"There's more at *steak* here than your face and Bo's bottom," said McMoo gravely.

"My fellow members!" Sir Lawrence smiled and joined Seymour, Dicky and Albert as they rushed forward to greet their "moo-dered" friends. "You are alive!"

But T-1901 raised his ray gun and snorted fire from his nostrils. "And now you will join them as part of my workforce."

McMoo frowned. "What are these poor slaves of yours doing, anyway?" He watched as the large black cow mooed  and wandered inside, heading for a cosy pen in the far corner of this secret nerve centre. "And how does it tie in with that enormous animal?"

Steam hissed from the robotic bull's horns. "Call that enormous? No. It must be bigger. Larger. GREATER. And with the help of you and your friends, it soon will be — ready to fight in a titanic army of killer cows!"

Chapter Nine

THINKING BIG

McMoo looked around the lab in horror. "You've been making your *moo-der* victims slave away here to help create that poor, oversized heifer?"

"Yes." T-1901 smiled. "These unfortunate fools have been creating a new type of cow-feed for me. A precise combination of plants that will cause any cow who eats it to swell to enormous size."

Sir Lawrence picked up some limp leaves and gasped in horror. "My prize pomp lilies are among them, I see!"

"Yes," T-1901 grated. "F.B.I. research indicated that pomp lilies had many unique properties. They are a vital ingredient of the cow-feed."

"And almost extinct even by 1851," said McMoo. "Which is why you set up your lab here, I suppose — next to a good supply!"

"And yet the correct combination of plants to achieve maximum cow growth has not been discovered." T-1901 smiled. "You will collaborate with your fellow prisoners. You will work without rest to create the cow-feed I require. If you do not have it ready within thirty-six hours . . . I will ter-moo-nate Queen Victoria!"

Eliza swooned, and Dicky clutched his chest so hard he almost fell over. Even the large cow looked mildly concerned.

"But . . . you can't!" Albert whined.

"Yes, I can, my princely friend," T-1901 assured him. "And now I have

lured you all here, I shall go to see her
right away."

Albert pushed out his chin defiantly.
"She'll run a mile as soon as she spots
you!"

The ter–moo–nator shook his head.
"I told you I am a master of illusion.
Behold . . ." He held up a golden nose
ring, then slotted it into his snout. The
air around him shimmered . . .

And the next moment, he looked exactly like Prince Albert!

"A ringblender with a built-in impersonation setting," McMoo marvelled. "Brilliant!"

"He still stinks of oil and bull-skin," Bo shouted.

"Your oh-so-British queen will be far too polite to comment." T-1901 tossed his ray gun to Fanny. "Guard them until I return. Your twin sister will join me and resume her work in the house – but she too will die if you try to defy me." He smiled at Sir Lawrence. "I will tell Victoria that urgent business has called you all back to London, but that you insisted we remained here where it was ... 'safe'."

"You diabolical demon!" cried Sir Lawrence.

"Just get on with your work," T-1901 snarled. "With your expertise and McMoo's genius, the task should be simple. So be ready by the day after tomorrow. Or else!"

The ter-moo-nator stalked away with Eliza struggling in his grip and the false wall swung down behind him.

"Quick, Professor," Bo hissed. "Now we can escape!"

Fanny fired the ray gun – and a bolt of energy smashed into the timber beam beside Bo's head.

"Or possibly not," Pat twittered.

"You heard old bully-boy," said Fanny, pointing the gun at Albert. "No tricks, and get working – all of you!"

"With innocent lives in danger, it's hopeless to resist, my friends," said one of the ragged botanists. "Come, all of you. Let us show you where we've got up to . . ."

The long hours passed for McMoo and his friends in a blur of chemicals and leaves, microscopes and stem-snippings, petals and pollen. They worked till they

were exhausted. Pat and Bo sat
miserably, tied up so tight they could
hardly move – and every time they did,
even just to scratch an itch, Fanny fired
a laser bolt in their direction.

Pat sighed. "She's a tough one. I don't
see any way out."

"She'll get tired in the end," Bo
whispered. "And when she does . . ."

"Don't try anything," Albert beseeched
them. "That evil man-bull might hurt
my little Vicki!" He checked his fob
watch and turned to Sir Lawrence.
"Twenty-four hours have gone already.

We only have until tomorrow morning!"

"Shut up!" hissed Fanny Barmer, an ear cocked to the far wall. "I hear something . . ."

The posh tones of Queen Victoria carried to them faintly. "These grounds are so lovely to stroll in. Such a pity that Sir Lawrence and his friends had to leave so soon after arriving. What *could* their urgent business be?"

"I really don't know, my dear," came the voice of T-1901 impersonating Albert. "But I trust they shall finish it soon and return."

The voices faded as the queen and her sinister companion walked on. Albert sighed, and the botanists hung their heads. The giant cow mooed.

"We'd better keep at it," the professor murmured.

★ ★ ★

The day turned to night as the hours went on crawling by. McMoo and the men worked flat out without food or sleep. Bo and Pat nibbled on scraps of grass and hay when no one was looking.

"Just half an hour to go till morning," Fanny yawned with a nasty smile. "Time's running out. Looks like Great Britain's going to need a new queen."

"Not so!" cried McMoo, leaping up from his microscope in a shower of peach blossom. "Dicky, that last cutting you added to the mixture might just be the one to do it."

Sir Lawrence stared at him, red-eyed and haggard. "Then let us test it, sir!"

As McMoo carried a big sack of new improved big-cow cow-feed over to the ter-moo-nator's giant pet, the other botanists held their breaths. One or two forgot to let their breath go again and quickly collapsed to the floor. But the

others barely noticed – and even Fanny
Barmer just stared, fascinated – as the
cow began to eat . . . and eat . . .

Pat and Bo looked nervously at
the professor. The professor looked
at Seymour. Seymour looked at Sir
Lawrence. Sir Lawrence looked at Albert.
Albert looked at Dicky. Dicky looked
unwell.

The big cow finished her meal and
stuck out her tongue. Then she lay down
heavily.

Seymour Bushes buried his head in his
hands. "It didn't work!"

With a sudden whirr, the stable wall
slid upwards to reveal the ter–moo–nator,
dressed in Albert's pyjamas. "Well?" he
demanded.

"They've failed," cried Fanny. "The
cow's no bigger."

T–1901's face darkened. His chimney
horns started pumping smoke and his
borrowed pyjamas started to singe. "You

dare to disappoint me?"

"Wait!" Pat gasped. "Look – something's happening!"

The cow was beginning to shake. Her hide was glowing an eerie red. With a weird, gurgling *moo*, she raised her head – and went on raising it! Her neck stretched out like a giraffe's – then the rest of her body began to catch up. She grew taller and taller, bigger and wider, crashing through the rotten ceiling, towering over all in the pale dawn light.

"Behold," whispered T-1901 in wonder. "The Ultra-Cow."

"Moo," said the Ultra-Cow, looking confused.

"There. You've got your giant heifer," said McMoo grimly.

Bo nodded. "But she's not exactly savage and war-like, is she?"

"Not yet. But observe." T-1901 pulled a small device from inside his pyjamas. "This transmits a special signal on cow frequencies. To ordinary cattle it is simply a nuisance. But to the enormous ears of an Ultra-Cow . . ."

He pressed a switch on the device.

"I hear nothing," said Sir Lawrence, and the other botanists agreed. But McMoo winced, Pat and Bo shook their heads — and the giant-sized Ultra-Cow started snarling and spitting and stamping her feet, mooing like a foghorn.

"You see?" laughed T-1901. "It drives her wild . . ." He tossed the device to the floor in front of Dicky Hart. With a growl of outrage and a moo of *cow*-trage, the Ultra-Cow lifted her hoof over Dicky's head, ready to bring it crashing down. The botanist screamed . . .

But then McMoo dived forward head over heels, scooped up the device, and hurled it into the pen.  The Ultra-Cow's hoof stamped down on it, squashing it flat.

At once, the giant animal was quiet and calm again.

"Perfect," hissed T-1901. "The Ultra-Cow will do anything to stop the signal. And I will place an identical device in Queen Victoria's crown, ready for when she opens the Great Exhibition later today!"

"The exhibition!" Albert spluttered. "I'd almost forgotten."

"So *that's* your plan," McMoo realized. "You'll switch on your signalling device and the Ultra-Cow will hear it, freak out and go charging into London to stop it – destroying Crystal Palace, the queen, hundreds of inventions and thousands of visitors from all over the world!"

"Correct," agreed T-1901. "The first event in a cow destruction spree that will bring the world to its knees ..."

Pat looked anxiously at Bo. "Leaving it ripe for a takeover by the F.B.I.!"

"I am grateful for your help, gentlemen," T-1901 told McMoo and the botanists. "Thanks to you, the human race is doomed." He began to laugh. "Let the Age of Evil Cows begin!"

Chapter 10

A CLASH OF GIANT UDDERS

T-1901's sinister laughter went on for several minutes. "I think I preferred the signal," Pat muttered.

Finally, the ter-moo-nator controlled himself. "I must leave you now. The Great Exhibition opens at three. My 'wife' and I must proceed from the Palace at noon. But while I am gone, you must create more of the cow-feed, so that I may create more Ultra-Cows. If you refuse, or try to escape, Fanny will ter-moo-nate you."

"Yes, an' then I'll zap you with this gun an' all!" the big Barmer said fiercely.

"What happens if your big cow gets

restless before you're ready?" McMoo enquired. "She'll bring the whole place down."

"I have prepared a giant cow-leg manacle to hold her here." T-1901 pulled a huge shackle and chain from under a bale of hay in the pen and clamped it around the ankle of the unprotesting cow. Then he turned to Fanny. "When she hears the signal and grows angry she will soon break free – but you will have time to reach safety."

"I'd better," Fanny growled.

"Now farewell, fools," T-1901 clanked away. "I will return only once the centre of London has been udderly destroyed . . ."

"Don't rush back on our account," McMoo called after him. There was no reply. A stunned hush settled over the stables.

"What can we do now?" asked Pat quietly.

"You can make more of that cow-feed stuff," Fanny snapped. "All of you — get on with it!"

More miserable hours passed, as McMoo and the botanists worked in stoic silence.

But then, suddenly, Bo nudged her brother. "The thing about eating lots is that, sooner or later, it all has to come out . . ."

Pat glanced at the Ultra-Cow. Her eyes were closed and she seemed to be straining a bit. "Uh-oh! Things could get smelly."

Bo nodded. "And if I time things just

right, they could get *extra* smelly for Barmer . . ."

"Stop that yakking!" snapped Fanny.

But just then, Seymour Bushes stifled a noisy sob. "It's no use." He sniffed loudly. "I can't go on."

"Nor I," said Dicky. "My heart is too heavy." He held his stomach. "Look, it's down here, I'm sure it is."

"Don't be so wet!" Fanny turned from Bo and aimed the gun at the botanists instead. "The next person to sob gets a—"

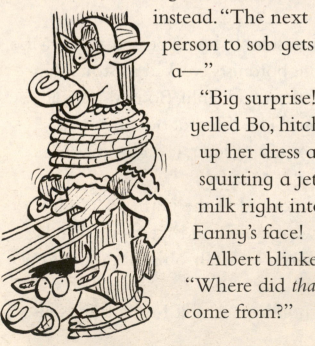

"Big surprise!" yelled Bo, hitching up her dress and squirting a jet of milk right into Fanny's face!

Albert blinked. "Where did *that* come from?"

Bo quickly covered her udder. "Where did *what* come from?" she asked innocently.

With a burbling cry, Fanny staggered back under the Ultra-Cow's hind legs . . .

Just in time to receive one of the biggest pats on the head in history.

SQUELCH! An avalanche of steaming dung fell over Fanny, knocking the gun from her grip. She shrieked as the huge dollops pinned her to the ground, and a ragged cheer went up from the botanists.

"Direct hit!" McMoo cried. He started to untie Pat and Bo, glancing up warily at the enormous beast. "Nice shooting, Bo," he whispered.

"We may have won a battle but the war is surely lost," said Albert forlornly. "That beastly bull will be in London by now. We can't stop him from sending his signal – and we certainly can't stop the Ultra-Cow."

"But if we can perfect an antidote and turn her back to normal, she won't be able to do any harm!" McMoo grinned. "And I dunno about you lot, but I've secretly been working on one all morning."

"Ingenious, my dear Professor," said Sir Lawrence. "Have you succeeded?"

"Not yet," McMoo admitted. "I need a plant with a bit more pizzazz. Something rich in vitamin Z . . ."

"Twenty-sixth-century clover!" Bo cried, pulling the wilted leaves from her pocket. "That's full of the stuff!"

"Genius!" McMoo declared, swiping the plant. "It might just work . . ."

But suddenly, the Ultra-Cow flicked its ears and started to growl. McMoo and Bo gasped, and Pat found he could hear a distant buzzing in his brain.

"T-1901's signal!" he breathed. "It's started transmitting!"

"And my antidote's not ready!" groaned McMoo. "We've got to calm down that cow."

Dicky looked around at his friends. "Anyone know any cow lullabies?"

"How about, 'Please, Big Cow, Don't Squash and Kill Us'?" suggested Seymour.

"*MOOOOO!*" With an ear-splitting cry, the Ultra-Cow broke free of her shackles.

"Someone's got to stop that thing," Bo
declared. "And since the special feed was
made for milk-cows, there's only one
chick qualified for the job."

"Bo, no," McMoo warned her. "It's too
dangerous."

The Ultra-Cow raised her head and
roared again. "So's that thing!" said Bo.
"Hey everyone – look over there!"

She pointed across the stable, and
while Albert and the
botanists turned
to see, she
whipped out her
ringblender, tore
off her human
clothes and
guzzled down
great gulpfuls of the
freshly created cow-feed.

"Where'd that heifer come from?"
cried Sir Lawrence. "And where's Miss
Vine?"

"She'll be all right," said McMoo, leaping clear of the Ultra-Cow's giant hoof. "I hope!"

"It's working," Bo mooed through a mouthful of feed. She could feel her whole body fizz with a billion bubbles. Her legs began to stretch, her head inflated like a balloon. Her udder swelled to resemble the world's largest blancmange as she grew, and grew and *grew* . . . "Whoaaa, this is amazing!"

Pat gulped, staring up at her in alarm. "Looks like my big sister just got bigger!"

"Hello, down there!" Bo waved down at McMoo, Pat and the others. "Ouch." She covered her ears. "That signal's really annoying. It wouldn't be so bad if it had a bit of a bass line, but . . ."

"*MOOO!*" Enraged by the signal, the Ultra-Cow reared up and swatted Bo into the stable wall.

"Ooh, my ticker!" groaned Dicky, as he and the other botanists ran for cover.

"Don't trash the lab, Bo!" McMoo yelled, working feverishly over a hot test tube. "Or I'll never be able to finish the antidote."

Bo was too busy dodging another hoof to hear him. "I don't want to hurt you," she mooed at the Ultra-Cow. "Just calm down!"

But the humongous heifer reared up and sprayed a giant jet of milk at Bo. Bo fought back with a blast of her own.

A tidal wave of milk crashed down over the lab, half-drowning Albert, Pat and the botanists.

McMoo wiped the milk from his eyes and glowered up at Bo. "You're not making this very easy!"

"Sorry, Prof," Bo called, grabbing the Ultra-Cow in a neck lock. "Just get a shift on – I can't hold her much longer!" The Ultra-Cow bucked and shook and kicked to be free, smashing down walls and snapping tables like twigs.

"Pat, clear the area!" cried McMoo. Covered in milk and straw, Pat led Albert and the terrified botanists away from the ruined stable. Only the professor remained, standing in the shambles, emptying the test tube over the twenty-sixth-century clover. "And get Fanny out of here too. She may be a ratbag but we can't let her be squashed."

Even as he spoke, the Ultra-Cow booted Fanny Barmer and sent her

streaking through the air like a human dungball. "Whoops!" McMoo leaped aside as she whistled past and crashed into a cupboard.

"The signal's driven this cow gaga!" hollered Bo desperately. "I can't stop her!"

The Ultra-Cow finally broke free and bent down, ready to suck up McMoo into her giant, dribbling jaws . . .

Chapter 11

CHAOS AT COW-RYSTAL PALACE

McMoo watched helplessly as the Ultra-Cow thrust its huge head towards him . . .

But then a dark shadowy shape suddenly appeared out of nowhere in front of the giant beast's face.

"The Black Cow of Doom!" Pat cried.

McMoo nodded. "Fanny must've set off the brooch when she hit the cupboard. Right now it could be just what we need!"

The Ultra-Cow's huge eyes followed the projection curiously as it danced and spun and spiralled. Her breathing grew deeper. She smiled sleepily.

"It's hypnotizing her!" Bo declared.

"Keep watching a minute longer," McMoo muttered, stirring in some fresh straw to his planty concoction. "Long enough for me to feed you . . . THIS!"

He hurled the batch of cow-feed into the drooling dairy-beast's mouth. Still entranced by the spinning spectre, the Ultra-Cow chewed automatically.

Pat crossed his hooves. McMoo held his breath. Bo accidentally knocked down a tree with her tail.

And then, with the sound of a deflating balloon, the Ultra-Cow started to shrink. Broken from her trance, she looked around in confusion as her body sagged and billowed, growing smaller ever faster. Finally, with a contented moo, she returned to normal size, and wandered off innocently to munch some grass.

"You did it, Professor!" Pat cheered. "You made the antidote."

"Now give some to me," called Bo. "That stupid signal is giving me earache!"

"I'm afraid I can't, Bo," McMoo told her. "Not just yet. Because if T-1901's giant cow doesn't show up to destroy the Crystal Palace, he might just decide to try it himself."

Pat frowned. "Of course! Disguised as Albert he could still ter-moo-nate Queen Victoria and the whole Royal Family – totally changing history!"

Bo groaned
so loudly that
the only
stable wall
still standing
fell apart
– revealing
Albert, Sir
Lawrence and

Dicky Hart creeping cautiously back
towards the lab – with Eliza Barmer.

"We did it, gents!" McMoo beamed.
"And lady. Hello, Eliza, where'd you
spring from?"

"That brutish bull locked me up in a
cupboard before he left with the queen,
but I managed to break free," said Eliza.
"Gracious!" she declared when she saw
– and smelled – the mess in the stable.
"You've dealt with my evil twin!"

Sir Lawrence looked up at Bo. "But
while we've lost one Ultra-Cow, we've
gained another . . ."

"This one is far friendlier," McMoo assured them. "She'll follow that signal straight to the Crystal Palace and take all of us with her."

"But this new cow is a different colour," Dicky pointed out. "The bull will know at once his plans have been thwarted, somehow."

"And he will harm my precious Vicki!" Albert cried.

McMoo smiled. "Not if we're very, *very* clever . . ."

"Forget it!" Fanny Barmer jumped back to her feet in a shower of milk and cow muck and raised her dented ray gun. "I aim to collect my cash from that bull, and I know how to put things right. So – bye-bye, Professor . . ."

And before anyone could react, she pointed the weapon at McMoo and opened fire . . .

* * *

In the Crystal Palace in Hyde Park –
disguised as Prince Albert in splendid
formal dress – T-1901 sat impatiently
beside Queen Victoria. They had been
given special thrones in the entrance
hall, a man-made cavern of iron and
glass. It was so vast that the enormous
oak trees it housed barely brushed
the ceiling.

T-1901 surveyed the scene coldly. V.I.P.s and ambassadors from all over the world crowded the platform around them. The flags of all nations waved cheerily. Someone was belting out hymns on a huge organ, as a massive choir sung along. The music and voices joyfully rang out to the 600,000 people gathered in the park for the Great Exhibition's grand opening. *Soon, these patriotic fools will be squashed by my Ultra-Cow*, he thought happily.

Queen Victoria sniffed. "Have you been smoking, dearest?"

T-1901 quickly waved away the wisps of steam coming from his chimney-like horns. "Certainly not, my sweet. It's just your imagination . . ." He looked at the queen's golden crown and chuckled. The transmitter hidden inside it had been sending out his signal of doom for over an hour. Any minute now . . .

Suddenly, the ter-moo-nator grinned

to hear a commotion from the crowd. Seconds later, screams and yells could be heard over the heavenly music.

Queen Victoria shifted uncomfortably. "Probably just some poor people being silly. Ignore them."

But it was Victoria T-1901 chose to ignore. He jumped up in delight as a huge, dark shadow fell over the palace, blotting out the sunlight. The choir choked and gasped, the organist played all the wrong notes and the gathered crowds stared up in fear and bewilderment as a great black cow pressed its head against the glass roof, its slobbery breath clouding up the windows.

T-1901 jumped to his feet and laughed. "Yes, my Cow of Doom!" he boomed, much to the puzzlement of a nearby ambassador. "Complete your work. *Destroy* the Crystal Palace! DESTROY EVERYTHING!"

Chapter Twelve

MOOOOOOOOOOL BRITANNIA!

"Albert!" Victoria shrieked. "You must run, my darling – that cow must surely plan to moo-der you!"

T-1901 said nothing. The giant cow had lowered her head to reveal the Barmer woman perched on its neck.

The ray gun was jammed under one arm and she clutched a large suitcase in each hand. She jumped down, shattering a pane of glass and falling into the uppermost branches of a huge oak tree.

"Fanny!" barked the ter-moo-nator. "What's the meaning of this?"

"I'm sorry, sir!" the big woman called, sliding down the tree with her baggage as waves of anxious chatter swept through the glass-and-iron halls. "There's been a snag in your plans. I had to talk to you at once!"

Queen Victoria glowered at T-1901, still believing him to be Albert. "You seem very familiar with this woman!"

T-1901 ignored her. "Speak, my servant."

"It's all my dreadful sister's fault," Barmer panted, red-faced and sweating, knocking V.I.P.s aside with her heavy suitcases as she marched over to the ter-moo-nator. "You see, she tried to shoot Professor McMoo, but the gun barrel was so dented it blew up in her face – so, *I* came along instead. I'm actually *Eliza* Barmer . . ." She reached out and grabbed T-1901's ringblender. "And *you* are a big ugly bull!"

"How dare you be so rude to my husband, girl!" Victoria began. Then she shrieked as the illusion of Albert fizzled away and the clanking, fuming bull was revealed. Dukes and duchesses and lords and ladies scattered in alarm.

"Impossible," T-1901 scowled.

"If you think *that's* impossible, try this!" came a foghorn moo from above that only bovine ears could understand. "I'm not your Ultra-Cow – I'm Not-So-Little Bo Vine in a muddy disguise!"

Sir Lawrence peeped out from behind one of her ears. "My gardens will never be the same after this giant cow rolled in the flower beds – but it was worth it!"

Dicky Hart peered around the other ear. "We took water from the fountains to make the soil nice and sticky then patted it all over her to trick you!"

"And thank goodness we were in

time," Prince Albert declared, looking out from under Bo's big top lip.

"My love!" cried Victoria. "Albert, is it truly you?"

"It's him all right, Your Majesty!"
Seymour Bushes pushed out of Bo's
left nostril. "Now, let's all clobber that
mechanical man-bull in the name of the
Queen."

"Hurrah!" cheered the ten kidnapped
botanists, who'd been hanging onto Bo's
enormous tail all the time. In a ragged
scramble, the reunited Green Thumb
Club members jumped down to the glass
roof of the palace, ducked through the

broken panes and started climbing down the tree.

"No!" T-1901's chest furnace sizzled red with rage. "I shall still triumph." He pulled another ray gun from inside his iron hip and pointed it at the queen. "Prepare for ter-moo-nation!"

But just then, both Eliza's cases burst open – to reveal Pat in one and Professor McMoo in the other!

T-1901 staggered back in shock.

"You don't look pleased to see us," Pat noted. "Perhaps you'd prefer to see *this*!" He jammed the Black Cow projection brooch into the ter-moo-nator's nostril and switched it on. T-1901 went cross-eyed as the image of the ghost started swirling *inside* his cast-iron head!

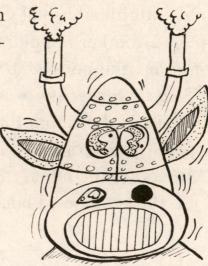

McMoo knocked the gun from the ter-moo-nator's grip. "And since I doubt you're pleased to *hear* us either, perhaps you'd prefer *this* little tune." He grabbed the crown from the speechless Queen Victoria and stuck a screwdriver into the secret signalling device. "If I can just change the frequency so it only affects computerized lugholes . . ."

"*Arrrgh!*" T-1901 clapped his hooves

over his ears so hard he put dents in them! "Signal too loud . . . Cannot bear . . ."

Prince Albert and the grimy botanists, like a gang of tatty Tarzans, reached the bottom of the tree and raced towards the ter-moo-nator. "Let's get him!" cried Dicky.

"He can't stop us all," agreed Sir Lawrence.

Pat grinned. "Right now, I don't think he can stop *any* of us!"

"Mission abort," groaned T-1901 pulling a portable time machine from his brick-red backside. "Abort . . ." He vanished in a cloud of black smoke before the botanists could reach him.

"We scared him off!" Seymour declared, as Prince Albert ran into the queen's arms. An enormous "ahhh" and a big cheer went up from the baffled, bewildered but now delighted crowd.

Pat turned to McMoo. "I'm glad

we won – but won't we have changed history by making this big entrance?"

McMoo pointed outside – big Bo had vanished. "Albert fed her the antidote when we got here – so she's turned back to normal now."

"But she walked for miles across London," Pat persisted. "Everyone saw her."

"This simply will not do," Victoria declared. "All this fuss and nonsense will overshadow my poor dear Albert's exhibition . . ." She cleared her throat noisily until the crowds fell silent. "Ladies and gentlemen, I am sorry for the curious incidents you have just witnessed. They were part of a fanciful prank played by Britain's enemies intended to spoil this Great Exhibition. But let us now show our enemies they have failed, by all agreeing never to breathe a single word of what has happened here today." She paused. "And kindly bear in mind, anyone who *does* will be transported to Australia for twenty years."

"Er, what *has* happened here, Your Majesty?" cried a nervous lord quickly. "I saw nothing."

"Nor I!" cried another, and another. "Nor I!" The chorus spread through the throughing British crowds.

"So without further ado, I declare this greatest of Great Exhibitions OPEN!" Queen Victoria declared to a flourish of trumpets and rousing cheers that shook the entire palace.

Sir Lawrence threw his arms around Seymour and clapped him heartily on the back.

The botanists skipped about the oak tree.

Dicky Hart grabbed Eliza and danced a jig. "The old ticker beats more strongly when I'm next to you," he confessed. "Eliza, will you marry me?"

"Oh, yes!" she whooped. "And my naughty sister shall become *our* housekeeper."

"Once she's cleared up the damage to Sir Lawrence's gardens, of course," Dicky agreed.

The queen waved happily at the jubilant crowds. "This is truly the most glorious day of our lives!"

"Job done," McMoo hissed in Pat's ear. "I think it's time we slipped quietly away to the present . . . "

* * *

Bo was waiting for Pat and the professor by the Time Shed. The crowds were too busy celebrating, singing and carefully not talking about giant heifers to notice a normal-sized cow in their midst.

"Well, the F.B.I. lab at Sir Larry's has been destroyed, the ter-moo-nator's defeated, history's back on track and the Great Exhibition's an instant success." McMoo puffed out a big breath. "I'd say we've earned ourselves a breather back on the farm."

"But when Bessie Barmer finishes the big Victorian extension to the farmhouse she'll be able to watch us all the time," Pat realized glumly.

"It'll be horrid," Bo agreed, following them into the shed.

"Cheer up!" McMoo pulled a big red lever and energy fizzed and frothed through the Time Shed's engines. "Things have a way of working out for the best . . ."

The shed arrived back on the farm a split second after it had left. Bo opened the door and saw Bessie staggering towards the half-built tower with a huge bundle of tools in her arms.

"The old ratbag should watch where she's going," Pat muttered.

"She should," McMoo agreed, "but I hope she doesn't – because she's heading straight for . . ."

"*Argh!*" Bessie yelled as she suddenly sank into something grey and sludgy.

"Wet cement!" She tried to get out, but the tools were weighing her down. "Help!" Dropping the tools into the sticky gloop, she strained to free one leg – but slipped over on her giant bottom and crashed into the scaffolding. "Oh, no!" she wailed as the whole tower collapsed beside her in an explosion of brick-dust and concrete.

Bo stifled a giggle. "It's such a shame we're stupid, ordinary cows, isn't it? Otherwise we could help."

Pat nodded. "What a shame!"

"Told you things would work out." McMoo grinned as he rushed to switch the kettle on. "Now, let's quickly report in to Yak, then follow the example of our Victorian friends and brew up for a right royal C.I.A. celebration."

Pat fetched the mugs. "With you around, Professor, they should call it the *Tea*-I-A!"

"Or how about the Tea-In-Hay?" Bo suggested.

"We are *NOT* a-moo-sed," said McMoo firmly – and then he laughed. "All right, then, yes we are. And with all of history to romp about in, we always will be – wherever and whenever we end up next!"

THE END

The Cows In Action
will return soon in

THE MOO-LYMPIC GAMES

Coming Soon!

The Moo-lympic Games

Don't miss McMoo, Pat and Bo in their next exciting,
action-packed adventure!

Visit www.**stevecolebooks**.co.uk for fun, games, jokes, to meet the characters and much, much more!

Welcome to a world where dinosaurs fly spaceships and cows use a time-machine . . .

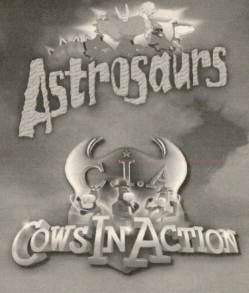

Sign up for the Steve Cole monthly newsletter to find out what your favourite author is up to!

THE UDDERLY MOOVELLOUS JOKE BOOK

by Steve Cole

What goes 'oom oom'?
A cow walking backwards!

What do you get if you sit under a cow?
A pat on the head!

With the F.B.I. working on a joke so funny it's *deadly*, McMoo, Pat and Bo set out on their most hilarious mission yet . . . They travel through time, revisiting the sites of their most exciting adventures, in search of the best – and worst – jokes ever . . . Jam packed full of great gags, witty wisecracks and perfect puns, this *Udderly Moo-vellous C.I.A. Joke* Book will have you chuckling and chortling for hours!

ISBN: 978 1 862 30882 4

Visit the coolest school in space!

ASTROSAURS ACADEMY

Destination: Danger!
by Steve Cole

Young Teggs Stegosaur is a pupil at ASTROSAURS
ACADEMY – where dinosaurs train to be
ASTROSAURS. With his best friends Blink and Dutch
beside him, amazing adventures and far-out fun are
never far away!

Arriving at the Academy,
the new astro-cadets face
their first mission – to
camp out in a deserted
space wilderness and
bring back something
exciting for show-and-
tell. But the sneaky tricks
of a rival team mean big
trouble for Teggs, Blink
and Dutch – especially
when a T.rex ship crash-
lands close by with a
VERY hungry crew . . .

ISBN: 978 1 862 30553 3